THOMAS
& FRIENDS™

Misty Island
RESCUE

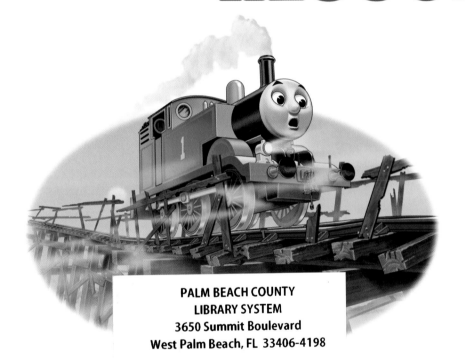

Illustrated by Tommy Stubbs

A GOLDEN BOOK · NEW YORK

Thomas the Tank Engine & Friends™

CREATED BY BRITT ALLCROFT

Based on The Railway Series by The Reverend W Awdry.
© 2010 Gullane (Thomas) LLC.
Thomas the Tank Engine & Friends and Thomas & Friends are trademarks of Gullane (Thomas) Limited.
HIT and the HIT Entertainment logo are trademarks of HIT Entertainment Limited.

All rights reserved. Published in the United States by Golden Books, an imprint of Random House Children's Books, a division
of Random House, Inc., 1745 Broadway, New York, NY 10019, and in Canada by Random House of Canada Limited, Toronto.
Golden Books, A Golden Book, and the G colophon are registered trademarks of Random House, Inc.

ISBN 978-0-375-86714-9 (trade) — ISBN 978-0-375-96714-6 (lib. bdg.)

www.randomhouse.com/kids   www.thomasandfriends.com

Printed in the United States of America

10 9 8 7 6 5 4 3 2 1

HiT entertainment

It was an exciting day on the Island of Sodor.
Construction was nearly complete on the new Search
and Rescue Center, which would help people in trouble.
There would be a new helipad for Harold, and Rocky was
getting his own shed. So there was much work to do.

"It will be made of the strongest wood of all—jobi wood," Sir Topham Hatt told Thomas and the other engines. "The wood will arrive today at Brendam Docks. The most useful engine at the end of the day will get to pull the jobi logs to the Search and Rescue Center."

Thomas went quickly to work.

Diesel wanted to show off. So with a biff and a bash, he shunted all the jobi wood away from the Docks.

"Stop!" Thomas puffed, his boiler bubbling.

Diesel only went faster and faster.

Unfortunately, the heavy flatbeds holding the wood jumped off the track and pulled Diesel towards the edge of a steep cliff. Thomas wasted no time pulling Diesel back to safety—but all the rich red wood tumbled into the sea.

Sir Topham Hatt was very pleased with Thomas. "You made the right decision to pull Diesel back. You didn't wait to be asked or to be told." As a reward, Thomas would visit the Mainland and bring back more jobi wood.

The next day, while Thomas waited to be loaded onto a ship, Salty told him and Percy about Misty Island.

"It's a mysterious place," Salty huffed. "Once an engine was lost there. No one could find him because of the mist."

"If I were lost on Misty Island," Thomas peeped, "I'd puff three times."

"I'd come save you," Percy promised.

The Dock Manager informed Thomas that there was no room for him on the ship. Thomas would have to wait for the next boat. But then Thomas spotted a raft.

"The ship can pull me on that," Thomas puffed.

Percy was worried that the raft wasn't safe.

"Don't worry. Sir Topham Hatt said I make the right decisions," assured Thomas.

And with that, the ship set out for the Mainland, pulling Thomas on a raft.

When Thomas was far out at sea and darkness started to fall, he heard a creak and a crash. The chain to the steamship had snapped. Thomas whistled and *wheesh*ed as the big boat steamed away, but no one could hear him. The rocking waves carried Thomas into the misty night.

The next morning, Thomas found himself on an unfamiliar island. It was quiet and very misty. As Thomas explored, he heard strange sounds. Rusty wheels rattled on old rails, and wild whistles echoed all around him.

Thomas called out, but no one answered. Then, as Thomas rounded a bend, he made an amazing discovery. . . .

Thomas had come fender-to-fender with three of the strangest engines he'd ever seen. "Cinders and ashes!" peeped Thomas. "Who are you?"

The strange engines' names were Bash, Dash, and Ferdinand. They told Thomas that he was on Misty Island.

"We're the Logging Locos," said Dash. "We've been watching you since you first rolled onto the island."

"We played Rattling Wheels and Whistling Whistles with you," Bash said. "But you didn't play with us. You can now if you want."

Thomas didn't want to play with Bash, Dash, and Ferdinand. Their games were strange.

"No thank you. I have to get back to the Island of Sodor."

And with that, Thomas *wheesh*ed backwards down the track.

Later, as the mist grew thicker and darkness fell, Thomas wasn't feeling so brave. He had chuffed and huffed all day, but he hadn't found a way off Misty Island. Thomas knew he would have to ask the Logging Locos for help.

The next morning, on Sodor, Sir Topham Hatt learned that Thomas was missing. Everyone wanted to help find Thomas. The engines searched all over Sodor. Harold took to the air. Sir Topham Hatt and Captain chugged out to sea.

Thomas spent the day looking for the Logging Locos. Tracks crissed and crossed. They climbed into foggy mountains and dove into tangled forests. Then, overlooking a deep valley, Thomas discovered an old logging camp.

"Footplates and fenders!" Thomas exclaimed. "I've found the Logging Locos." Bash, Dash, and Ferdinand were loading wood in the old logging camp. Thomas asked them for help, but they were busy.

"We said hello to you yesterday," Dash said. "But you didn't want to be friends with us."

"I'm sorry," Thomas peeped. "I was silly to think I could find a way off Misty Island by myself."

Then Thomas realized something amazing. "Bumpers and buffers! These logs are jobi logs! That's the wood we need to build the Search and Rescue Center!"

The Logging Locos clanked closer together to listen as Thomas told them about the Rescue Center. They agreed to help him collect logs.

Thomas showed the Locos how quickly he could shunt flatbeds holding logs. "One biff, one bash, and there's never a crash."

"We can't work this hard," said Dash.

"We'll run out of oil," said Bash.

"That's right," added Ferdinand.

The Logging Locos weren't diesels, but they used wood and oil for fuel.

"I'm sure you have enough oil," Thomas reassured them. "Sir Topham Hatt says I make good decisions."

The engines busily hauled logs and shunted flatbeds. But when they came to a rickety old bridge, Thomas stopped. The Logging Locos liked bouncing on the wibbly, wobbly Shake Shake Bridge.

"Yippee!" they cheered as they chugged across the quaking tracks.

Thomas didn't like the bridge, but he knew he had to cross it to collect the jobi wood. So, wobbly wheel by wobbly wheel, he crept slowly across.

Everything shook—but nothing broke—and Thomas was proud of himself for being so bold and brave.

Thomas needed to load the heavy logs onto flatbeds, but Ol' Wheezy, the camp's giant log loader, wasn't much help. He liked throwing logs instead of loading them.

He jiggled and joggled and spun.

Logs flew here and there. They splashed in a pond and crashed into trees. One even bashed Thomas on the boiler. The Locos cackled with laughter.

Thomas needed a better way to load the jobi wood. Luckily, he spotted an old machine.

"That's Hee Haw," said Dash. "He's the old log-loading machine."

"He needs too much oil," Bash added. "That's why we don't use him."

Thomas wasn't worried. They poured the last of the oil into Hee Haw. As the old machine creaked and sputtered into action, Thomas was very pleased.

Soon Thomas had three flatbeds full of jobi logs,
but he had no idea how to get them back to Sodor.
"We could use the tunnel," Dash suggested.
Thomas was amazed. "You didn't tell me there
was a tunnel to Sodor," he peeped.
"That's because it's closed," Dash said.
"Because it's dangerous," Bash added.
Thomas was too excited to listen. "I know all
about tunnels. It won't be dangerous."

The engines wheezed and *wheesh*ed to the old tunnel. Dash stopped at the entrance.

"We Locos don't have enough oil to puff to Sodor," he said.

"Of course you do," puffed Thomas as he pushed his flatbed into the tunnel. "It's just a whir and a whiff, and we'll be there."

They all disappeared into the dark and twisty tunnel.

Suddenly, there was trouble ahead. The tracks were blocked by rocks. Then, with a rumble and a crash, more rocks smashed down behind them.

"We can push the rocks out of the way," Thomas puffed.

Bash, Dash, and Ferdinand bravely pumped their pistons, but with a gasp and a groan, they ran out of oil. They couldn't push anymore.

The engines were stuck in the tunnel . . . and no one knew where they were.

Just then, Ferdinand noticed something. "I feel air on my funnel," he peeped.

Dash spotted a hole in the roof of the tunnel.

"Puff forward, Thomas—and huff your hardest," Bash suggested. "Someone will see your steam."

Thomas excitedly beamed from buffer to buffer and started to puff.

Back at Brendam Docks, Percy saw something that
made his firebox fizz. Three puffs of steam floated high
in the distance.

"It's Thomas!" Percy peeped. "He's on Misty Island,
and he needs help!"

Percy told Sir Topham Hatt and all the engines about Thomas. Everyone was ready to help.

"James, Gordon, and Edward, you will sail to Misty Island with me," said Sir Topham Hatt.

Then Whiff suggested using the abandoned tunnel that led to Misty Island. "It would be the fastest way to reach Thomas."

"Won't that be dark and dangerous?" asked Sir Topham Hatt.

"Don't worry," puffed Whiff. "I know all the tracks."

Meanwhile, Thomas and the Logging Locos were waiting in the dark tunnel. Soon they heard a noise coming through the rocks. It was the *clickety-clack* of wheels on the tracks. Then Thomas recognized Percy's friendly voice.

"Whiff and I have found you, Thomas!" peeped Percy.

"Watch out, Thomas," Whiff puffed. "Percy and I are going to push through the rocks to reach you."

With that, Percy and Whiff rocked and rolled backwards together. Then they pumped their pistons and crashed through the rocks.

"Hooray for Percy!" puffed Thomas. "Hooray for Whiff!"

Thomas introduced Whiff and Percy to the Logging Locos.

With a shove and a shunt, Whiff pulled the brave engines out of the tunnel. The Logging Locos *wheesh*ed and *whoosh*ed with wonder when they saw the sunny Island of Sodor.

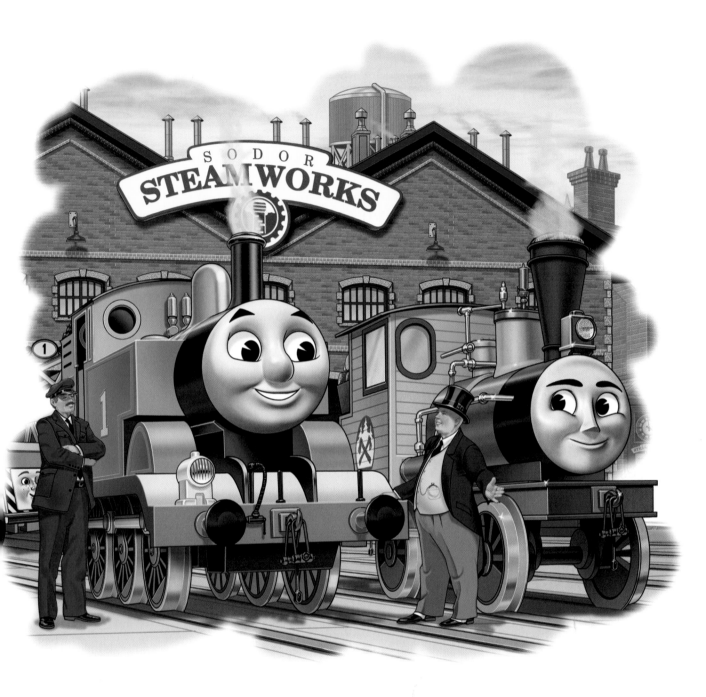

Thomas helped the Logging Locos to the Sodor
Steamworks for repairs. He knew that Kevin and Victor
would make them good as new.

Sir Topham Hatt was excited to see that Thomas was
safe—and that with all the jobi wood Thomas had found
on Misty Island, the Rescue Center would be finished in
no time.

Finally, the big day arrived: The Sodor Search and Rescue Center and the Misty Island Tunnel were officially opened!

"Today is a very special day, made possible by very special engines," Sir Topham Hatt said as he cut a red ribbon with a giant pair of scissors.

The people cheered and the engines peeped. Thomas, surrounded by his old and new friends, beamed with pride.